Out of the Egg

Written by Brylee Gibson

Here are eggs.
They are in the sand.
They are tortoise eggs.

eggs

Look at the egg.
A tortoise is
in this egg.
He will come out.

egg

Look!
A hole is in the egg.
The tortoise put the hole
in the egg.

hole

The tortoise
bites the egg.
He can see out
of the egg.

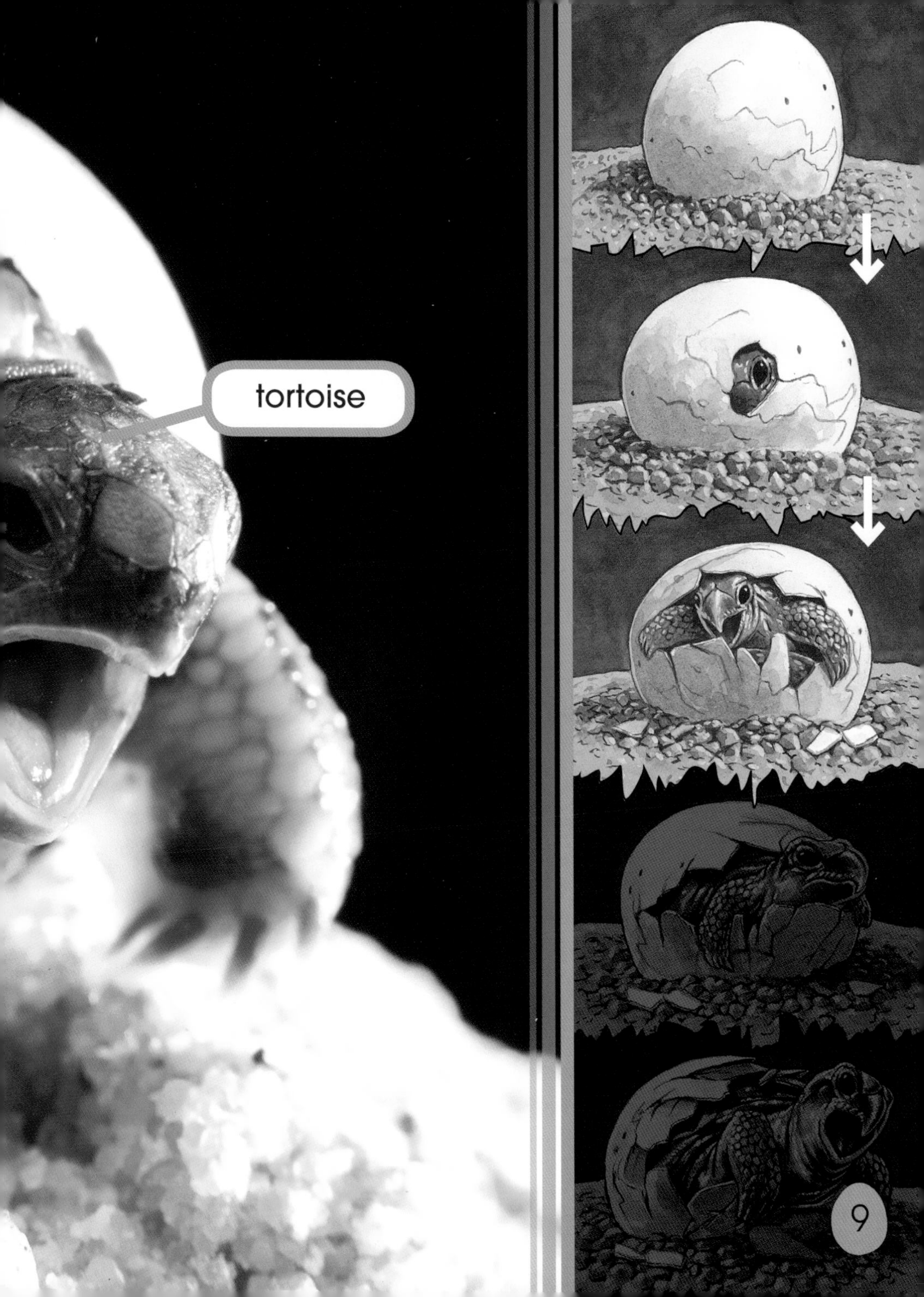
tortoise

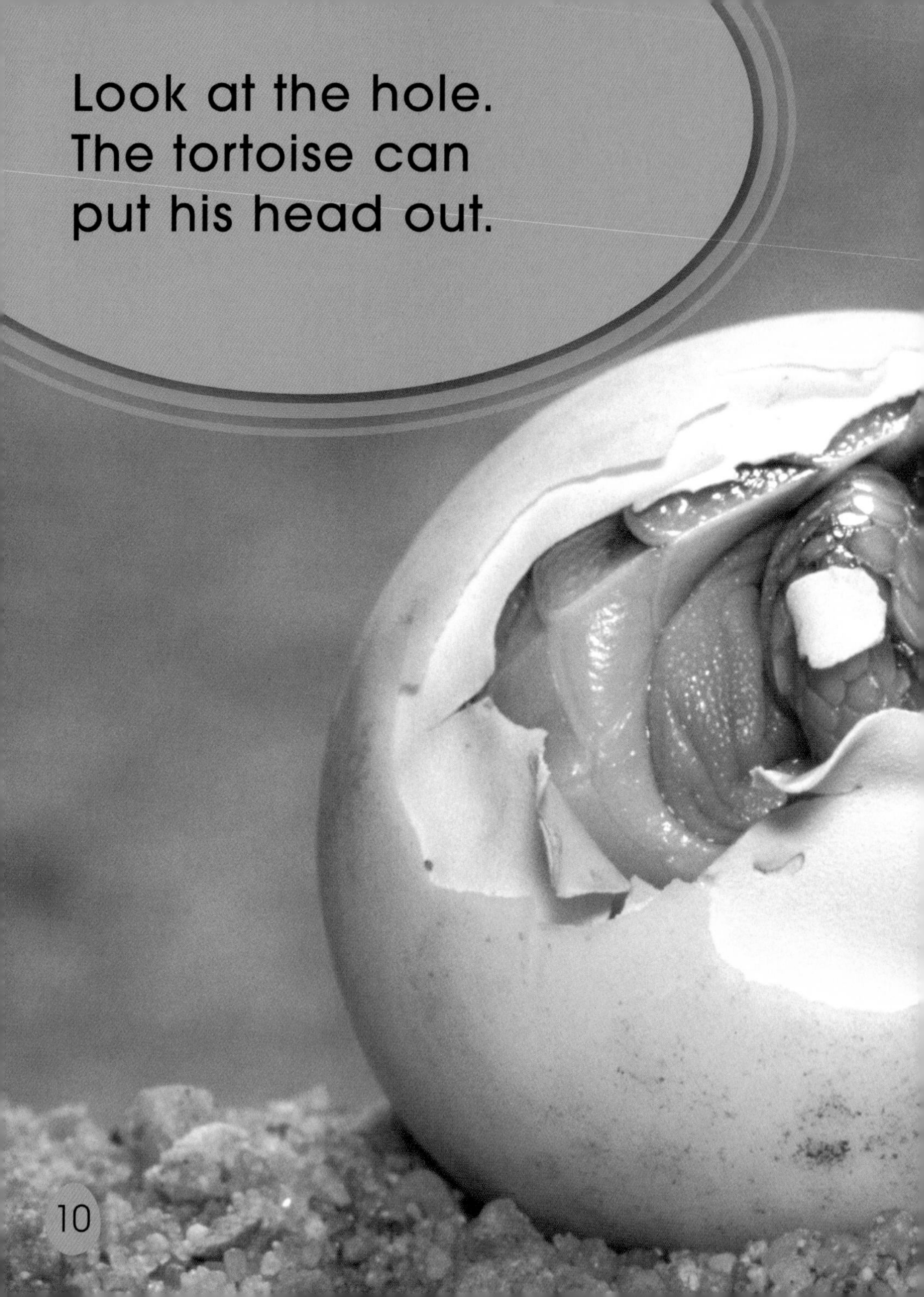

Look at the hole.
The tortoise can
put his head out.

The hole is big.
The tortoise can get
out of the egg.

The tortoise is
out of the egg.
He will go away
to get food.

Index

Guide Notes

Title: Out of the Egg
Stage: Early (2) – Yellow

Genre: Nonfiction
Approach: Guided Reading
Processes: Thinking Critically, Exploring Language, Processing Information
Written and Visual Focus: Photographs (static images), Index, Labels, Diagrams
Word Count: 90

Thinking Critically

(sample questions)

- Look at the title and read it to the children.
- Ask the children what they know about how animals come out of eggs.
- Focus the children's attention on the index. Ask: "What are you going to find out about in this book?"
- If you want to find out about tortoise eggs in the sand, which page would you look on?
- If you want to find out about the tortoise getting out of an egg, which pages would you look on?
- What do you think makes the tortoise come out of the egg?
- What do you think could happen to the tortoise when it is out of the egg?

Exploring Language

Terminology

Title, cover, photographs, author, photographers

Vocabulary

Interest words: tortoise, egg, hole, food, bites, head
High-frequency words: his, away, get
Positional words: in, out

Print Conventions

Capital letter for sentence beginnings, periods, exclamation mark